7108

A Note to Parents and Caregivers:

Read-it! Readers are for children who are just starting on the amazing road to reading. These beautiful books support both the acquisition of reading skills and the love of books.

 The PURPLE LEVEL presents basic topics and objects using high frequency words and simple language patterns.

 The RED LEVEL presents familiar topics using common words and repeating sentence patterns.

 The BLUE LEVEL presents new ideas using a larger vocabulary and varied sentence structure.

 The YELLOW LEVEL presents more challenging ideas, a broad vocabulary, and wide variety in sentence structure.

 The GREEN LEVEL presents more complex ideas, an extended vocabulary range, and expanded language structures.

 The ORANGE LEVEL presents a wide range of ideas and concepts using challenging vocabulary and complex language structures.

When sharing a book with your child, read in short stretches, pausing often to talk about the pictures. Have your child turn the pages and point to the pictures and familiar words. And be sure to reread favorite stories or parts of stories.

There is no right or wrong way to share books with children. Find time to read with your child, and pass on the legacy of literacy.

Adria F. Klein, Ph.D.
Professor Emeritus
California State University
San Bernardino, California

Editor: Jill Kalz
Designers: Joe Anderson and Amy Muehlenhardt
Page Production: Melissa Kes
Art Director: Nathan Gassman
Associate Managing Editor: Christianne Jones
The illustrations in this book were created with watercolor and ink.

Picture Window Books
5115 Excelsior Boulevard
Suite 232
Minneapolis, MN 55416
877-845-8392
www.picturewindowbooks.com

Printed in the United States of America.

Library of Congress Cataloging-in-Publication Data
Healy, Nick.
The big pig / by Nick Healy ; illustrated by Ronnie Rooney.
p. cm. — (Read-it! readers)
Summary: When Uncle Pete takes Cliff and Henry to the state fair, they sample
their way through the longest hot dog, the fastest roller coaster, and the thickest
chocolate shakes, while on the way to see the biggest pig.
ISBN-13: 978-1-4048-3385-2 (library binding)
ISBN-10: 1-4048-3385-4 (library binding)
ISBN-13: 978-1-4048-3386-9 (paperback)
ISBN-10: 1-4048-3386-2 (paperback)
[1. Fairs—Fiction. 2. Uncles—Fiction. 3. Pigs—Fiction.] I. Rooney, Ronnie, ill.
II. Title.
PZ7.H34463Bi 2006
[E]—dc22   2006027277

The BIG Pig

by Nick Healy
illustrated by Ronnie Rooney

Special thanks to our advisers for their expertise:

Adria F. Klein, Ph.D.
Professor Emeritus, California State University
San Bernardino, California

Susan Kesselring, M.A.
Literacy Educator
Rosemount–Apple Valley–Eagan (Minnesota) School District

PICTURE WINDOW BOOKS
Minneapolis, Minnesota

Uncle Pete told his nephews about the treats they would find at the state fair. Henry tried not to giggle. Cliff rolled his eyes. Uncle Pete always talked about food.

"Don't forget the big pig," Cliff said. "Henry wants to see the big pig."

"Of course," Uncle Pete said. "How could we forget the big pig?"

Uncle Pete parked the car at the back of the biggest parking lot Henry had ever seen.

"Let's hurry," Uncle Pete said as he handed the boys their tickets. "I need a hot dog."

Uncle Pete bought a giant hot dog. It was as long as three normal hot dogs. He piled on relish. Then he squirted mustard on top. His first bite was huge, and mustard dripped onto his shirt. Cliff rolled his eyes.

"We had better keep moving, boys," Uncle Pete said with his mouth full. "The pig barn is all the way across the fairgrounds."

They walked through a crowd of people. Henry saw kids standing in a long line. They were waiting to sit in the biggest tractor in the state.

Henry saw other kids lined up to ride the fastest roller coaster in the state.

13

He saw still more kids lined up to buy the thickest chocolate shakes in the state.

Uncle Pete got in line, too. He bought one large shake and two small ones.

Henry sucked on the straw, but nothing happened. He sucked and sucked until Cliff rolled his eyes again.

"That will never work," Cliff said.

"Use your spoon," Uncle Pete said. He scooped a huge spoonful into his mouth.

Uncle Pete and the boys finished their shakes while they waited in line at the Super Slide. The sign said it was the longest slide in the state. Uncle Pete and Cliff could hardly wait to go down. Henry wasn't so sure.

LONGEST SLIDE IN THE STATE

19

The top of the slide was like the top of the world.
Henry could see the whole fairgrounds.

He could hear bands playing and race cars roaring. He could smell pizza, french fries, and popcorn. He tried to find the pig barn.

"Let's race!" Cliff shouted.

Uncle Pete, Cliff, and Henry zoomed down the slide. The wind rushed past Henry's face. He yelled all the way down.

23

Uncle Pete won by a mile. Henry came in last, but he didn't mind. On the way down, he had spotted the pig barn.

"Who wants cheese chunks?" Uncle Pete asked.

"What about the pig barn?" Henry asked. "We're almost there."

"Cheese chunks come first," Cliff said.

This time, Henry rolled his eyes.

Uncle Pete let Cliff carry the bucket of cheese chunks. It was the biggest bucket they could get. They chewed quickly and walked slowly.

The cheese chunks were hot and slippery in Henry's hand. They were tasty in his mouth.

When Uncle Pete and the boys got to the pig barn, the big pig was asleep. His name was Orville, and he was the biggest pig in the state. He was as big as at least three Uncle Petes.

Henry leaned over the side of the pigpen for a better look. He whispered, "Hello, Orville."

"Hey, Henry!" Uncle Pete yelled, waking up the pig. "Smile!"

When Henry looked up, Uncle Pete snapped a picture. Henry's smile was the biggest smile in the state.

More *Read-it!* Readers

Bright pictures and fun stories help you practice your reading skills. Look for more books at your level.

Alex and Toolie
Another Pet
Bliss, Blueberries, and the Butterfly
Camden's Game
Cass the Monkey
Charlie's Tasks
Clever Cat
Flora McQuack
Kyle's Recess
Marconi the Wizard
Peppy, Patch, and the Postman
Peter's Secret
Pets on Vacation
The Princess and the Tower
Theodore the Millipede
The Three Princesses
Tromso the Troll
Willie the Whale
The Zoo Band

Looking for a specific title or level? A complete list of *Read-it!* Readers is available on our Web site:
www.picturewindowbooks.com